Dear Parents:

Congratulations! Your child is taking the first steps on an exciting journey. The destination? Independent reading!

STEP INTO READING® will help your child get there. The program offers five steps to reading success. Each step includes fun stories and colorful art or photographs. In addition to original fiction and books with favorite characters, there are Step into Reading Non-Fiction Readers, Phonics Readers and Boxed Sets, Sticker Readers, and Comic Readers—a complete literacy program with something to interest every child.

Learning to Read, Step by Step!

Ready to Read   Preschool–Kindergarten
• big type and easy words • rhyme and rhythm • picture clues
For children who know the alphabet and are eager to begin reading.

Reading with Help   Preschool–Grade 1
• basic vocabulary • short sentences • simple stories
For children who recognize familiar words and sound out new words with help.

Reading on Your Own   Grades 1–3
• engaging characters • easy-to-follow plots • popular topics
For children who are ready to read on their own.

Reading Paragraphs   Grades 2–3
• challenging vocabulary • short paragraphs • exciting stories
For newly independent readers who read simple sentences with confidence.

Ready for Chapters   Grades 2–4
• chapters • longer paragraphs • full-color art
For children who want to take the plunge into chapter books but still like colorful pictures.

STEP INTO READING® is designed to give every child a successful reading experience. The grade levels are only guides; children will progress through the steps at their own speed, developing confidence in their reading.

Remember, a lifetime love of reading starts with a single step!

Step into Reading, Random House, and the Random House colophon are registered trademarks
of Penguin Random House LLC.

Visit us on the Web!
StepIntoReading.com
rhcbooks.com

Educators and librarians, for a variety of teaching tools, visit us at RHTeachersLibrarians.com

ISBN 978-0-7364-4051-6 (trade)
ISBN 978-0-7364-8289-9 (lib. bdg.)
ISBN 978-0-7364-4052-3 (ebook)

Printed in the United States of America   10 9 8 7 6 5 4 3 2 1

DISNEY · PIXAR
ONWARD

A Day with Dad

by Susan Amerikaner

illustrated by the Disney Storybook Art Team

Random House 🏠 New York

Long ago, the world
was full of magic,
wizards, and wonder.
But over time,
things changed.

Ian Lightfoot is a regular elf.

He does not think about magic.

He is shy and unsure.

Ian's older brother, Barley,
wants magic to return.
He is loud and rough.

At school, Ian speaks
up for himself.
But nobody listens.

Ian takes a driving lesson.

He is afraid to drive

on the highway.

The cars move so fast!

Ian is sad.

He wants to be

bold, like his dad.

Dad died before Ian was born.

Ian looks at family photos.

He wants to meet Dad
more than anything.

Mom has a surprise.

Dad left a wizard's staff,

a Phoenix Gem, and a magic spell.

The spell can bring Dad back

to visit for one day!

Barley cannot wait to see Dad.

He grabs the staff and the gem.

He tries the spell

over and over,

but nothing happens.

Then Ian tries the spell.

The bottom half of Dad appears,

but the gem breaks!

The brothers must find another gem
to finish the spell before sunset.

Barley says they need
to see the Manticore.
She will know how to find
another gem.

The Manticore does not
want to help them.
Ian and Barley
must do it alone.

During their quest,
their van runs low on gas.
Their gas can
is almost empty, too.

Ian tries a spell to make
the gas can bigger.
Something goes wrong.
Barley shrinks instead!

They find a gas station.

Sprites are causing trouble there.

Dad bumps into their motorcycles.

This makes the sprites angry!

The sprites chase them.

Barley is now too small to reach

the steering wheel.

Ian must drive.

Barley helps Ian.

They get away!

Later, they arrive

at a bottomless pit.

Ian uses magic to cross it.

He is afraid, but with Barley's help,

they make it to the other side!

Ian, Barley, and Dad reach
an underground tunnel.
Ian uses a spell on one
of Barley's cheese puffs
to make a magic speedboat!

Ian and Barley end up
back in town.
The day is almost over,
and they still have no gem.
Their quest failed.

Then Barley finds a clue.

The Phoenix Gem is in town.

But red smoke appears.

The smoke turns into

a huge dragon!

Mom and the Manticore

arrive to help the boys.

They fight the dragon.

Ian finishes the spell
to bring Dad back.
But only one of the boys
can reach Dad in time.
Ian tells Barley to go
and see Dad.

Ian uses all the magic skills

he has learned.

He slays the dragon

and ends the curse!

Ian is trapped by rocks.

He sees Barley and Dad.

Dad hugs Barley.

The sun sets.

Dad disappears.

The Lightfoot brothers
will always have each other.
With a little magic,
they can do anything!